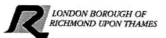
MARGAR
who sa
for childi
of the outstandin   varded
the Hans Christi   ational
recognition gr   oks.
Twice winner of t   become
modern class   ide
Dashing Dog, with   *andango*
and *Bul*

POLLY DUNE   Art,
and now lives and works in Brighton. She is the author
and illustrator of *Penguin, Dog Blue* and the Tilly books.
Her books for Frances Lincoln include *Looking After Louis*
and *Measuring Angels*, both written by Lesley Ely, as well as
The Man from the *Land of Fandango* and
Bubble Trouble with Margaret Mahy.

To those twin rascals Julia and Biddy... I have often tried
to find you down the back of the chair – M.M.

For Lucy Neale, with love – P.D.

Brimming with creative inspiration, how-to projects, and useful
information to enrich your everyday life, Quarto Knows is a favourite
destination for those pursuing their interests and passions. Visit our
site and dig deeper with our books into your area of interest:
Quarto Creates, Quarto Cooks, Quarto Homes, Quarto Lives,
Quarto Drives, Quarto Explores, Quarto Gifts, or Quarto Kids.

Down the Back of the Chair
Text copyright © Margaret Mahy 2006
Illustrations copyright © Polly Dunbar 2006

First published in 2006 by Frances Lincoln Children's Books.
This paperback edition first published in 2007 by
Frances Lincoln Children's Books, an imprint of The Quarto Group.
The Old Brewery, 6 Blundell Street, London N7 9BH, United Kingdom.
T (0)20 7700 6700 F (0)20 7700 8066 www.QuartoKnows.com

A catalogue record for this book is available from the British Library.

ISBN 978-0-7112-5398-8

Manufactured in Guangdong, China TT012020

9

FSC
www.fsc.org
MIX
Paper from
responsible sources
FSC® C016973

Down the Back of the Chair

Margaret Mahy

Illustrated by Polly Dunbar

Frances Lincoln
Children's Books

Our car is slow to start and go.
We can't afford a new one.
Now, if you please, Dad's lost the keys.
We're facing rack and ruin.

No car, no work! No work, no pay!
We're growing poorer day by day.
No wonder Dad is turning grey.
The morning is a blue one.

Nothing but dockets
in his pockets,
raging with despair,

Dad acts appalled!
Though nearly bald,
he tries to tear his hair.

But Mary,
who is barely two,
says, "Dad should do
what I would do!

I lose a lot, but I find a few —
down the back of the chair."

He's patted himself and searched the shelf.
He's hunted here and there,
so now he'll kneel and try to feel
right down the back of the chair.

Oh, it seemed to grin as his hand went in.
He felt tingling under his skin.
What will a troubled father win
from down the back of the chair?

Some hairy string and a diamond ring

were down the back of the chair.

Pineapple peel and a conger eel

were down the back of the chair.

A packet of pins and **one of the twins,** down the back of the chair.

A pan, a fan that belonged to Gran,

down the back of the chair...

A crumb,

a comb,

a clown,

a cap,

a pirate with a **treasure** map,

a dragon trying to take a nap —

down the back

of the chair.

A cake, a drake, a smiling snake,

down the back of the chair.

A string of pearls,
a lion with curls,
down the back
of the chair.

A skink, a skunk, a skate, a ski,

a couple of elephants

drinking tea,

a bandicoot and a bumblebee, down the back of the chair.

But what is this?

Oh, bliss! Oh, bliss!

Down the back of the chair.

The long lost will

of Uncle Bill,

down the back

of the chair.

His **money box** all crammed with cash,
tangled up in a scarlet sash.
There's **pleasure, treasure, toys** and **trash** -
down the back of the chair.

"I've found my dreams,"

our father beams,

"down the back of the chair.

At last I see

how life can be,

down the back

of the chair."

"Forget the keys! We're poor no more.
Just call a taxi to the door."

A taxi shot out with a roar

from down the back of the chair.

The chair
the chair,
the challenging chair,
the champion chair, the cheerful chair,
the charming chair, the children's chair,
the chopped and chipped, but chosen chair.
To think our fortune
waited there -
down the back
of the
chair!

MORE FANTASTIC PICTURE BOOKS BY MARGARET MAHY AND POLLY DUNBAR FROM FRANCES LINCOLN CHILDREN'S BOOKS

THE MAN FROM THE LAND OF FANDANGO

"Witty wordplay and beautiful illustrations" *Junior*

"A perfect book to read aloud"
Charlie Higson, the Mail on Sunday

"Fizzes with energy"
Bookseller

BUBBLE TROUBLE

"A huge adventure with laugh-out-loud text and gorgeous illustrations" – *Lovereading*

"A joy to read aloud" – *Bookseller*

"Never fails to delight" – *The Times*